Rockslide Rescue

Written by
Sandy Zaugg

Book 8
Created by
Jerry D. Thomas

Pacific Press® Publishing Association
Nampa, Idaho
Oshawa, Ontario, Canada

Edited by Jerry D. Thomas
Designed by Dennis Ferree
Cover art by Stephanie Britt
Illustrations by Mark Ford

Zaugg, Sandra L., 1938-
    The rockslide rescue / written by Sandy
Zaugg ; [inside illustrations by Mark Ford].
        p.   cm. — (The shoebox kids ; bk. 8)
    Summary: When Willie, who uses a wheelchair, and
his grandfather are caught in a landslide, some of the
other Shoebox Kids use Morse code in addition to
prayers to help find and rescue them. Includes
transcription of Morse code and instructions for
making a "buttertub" transmitter.
    ISBN 0-8163-1387-3 (pbk. : alk. paper)
    [1. Morse code. 2. Christian life. 3. Grandfathers.
4. Physically handicapped.] I. Ford, Mark, ill. II. Title.
III. Series.
PZ7.Z2675Ro   1998
—dc21   97-12883
                                                        CIP
                                                         AC

98 99 00 01 02 • 5 4 3 2 1

Contents

Other Books in The Shoebox Kids Series

The Mysterious Treasure Map
The Case of the Secret Code
Jenny's Cat-napped Cat
The Missing Combination Mystery
The Broken Dozen Mystery
The Wedding Dress Disaster
The Clue in the Secret Passage

Hi!

Wouldn't you like to know a secret code? Then you could send messages that only your friends would understand!

In this Shoebox Kids book, that's exactly what Willie, Chris, and Sammy do. They learn Morse code. And in this book, you can learn to build your own "buttertub transmitter" and send messages to your friends.

The Rockslide Mystery is written by my friend, Sandy Zaugg. She's created a story that will keep you on the edge of your seat worried and wondering what will happen next. But while you read about Willie and the danger he is in, you can learn some important lessons about trusting God.

Reading about Willie and the other Shoebox Kids is more than just fun—it's about learning what the Bible really means—at home, at school, or on the playground. If you're trying to be a friend of Jesus', then the Shoebox Kids books are just for you!

Jerry D. Thomas

P.S. If you enjoy the Shoebox Kids books or their stories in Primary Treasure, send me a message and let me know! You can send an e-mail message to jertho@pacificpress.com or write to me at The Shoebox Kids, P.O. Box 5353, Nampa, ID 83653.

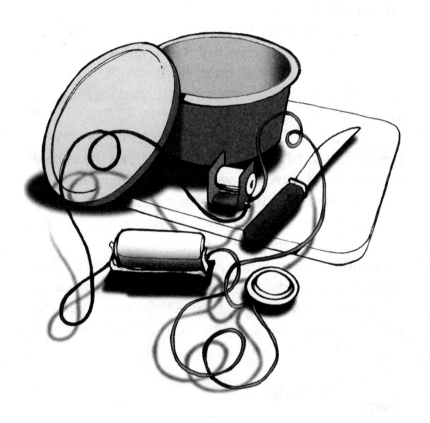

Buttertub Transmitters

"I bought the stuff!" Willie Taylor announced, happily waving a small plastic bag from Radio Shack as he entered Chris Vargas's home. "Now I can make a—a-sender too."

"A transmitter," Chris corrected, smiling. "You call it a transmitter. Sending a message is the same as transmitting a message." He led the way to the kitchen table where his electronic parts were waiting. "Dad wrote down the directions for us, and Sammy will be here soon. This is going to be great!"

Just a few weeks before, Chris and Sammy

had to write a report for social studies class. "When Sammy and I first read about Samuel Morse," Chris explained while they waited, "we thought he was boring. Then we found out about his secret code."

Willie didn't know the whole story. "Why did Samuel Morse need a secret code?" he asked.

Chris shrugged. "He wasn't really trying to keep a secret. But this was when there were no telephones. Morse invented the telegraph."

"What's a telegraph?" Willie asked.

"It's a way to send messages to someone a long way away by using a wire and a transmitter. The transmitter sends buzzes of sound. Samuel Morse created a special code using short buzzes and long buzzes so people could send messages to each other."

Willie pulled out a sheet of paper covered with dots and dashes. "So when you write Morse code on paper, the short buzzes must be the dots and the long buzzes must be the dashes."

"Right," Chris agreed. "And when you say them out loud, you say 'dit' for a dot and 'dah' for a dash."

Finally Sammy arrived, proudly holding up his plastic bag. "Hi, guys," he called. "I hope I got everything. That electronics store is a neat place. Did you see that computer program that helps you learn Morse code?" He dumped his stuff on the table by Willie's and Chris's.

"I saw that," Willie said. "That would be a great way to really get good at sending and understanding code messages. I wish I could buy it, but it cost more money than I've got. Oh, well, maybe I can drop hints about getting it for my birthday or Christmas."

Chris grabbed a small package and began to open it. "OK, let's get started! So this is 'Momentary (mo-men-tare-ee) Push-Button Soft-Feel Switch.' Wow, the name is bigger than the switch." Before long, each of them had a switch, a battery holder, and a little thing called a buzzer on the table in front of them.

Chris stared at his stuff. "My dad says this is easy. First, we connect the black wire from the buzzer and the black wire from the battery holder." He looked at his wires and frowned. "How can you do that?"

"Here, I got it," Willie said. He showed his wire connection to Chris. "Just bend the little wire ends into hooks and hook them together. See?"

"I got it," Sammy said, holding up the connected wires.

"I don't," Chris said, bending over his. "These
wires are so tiny they keep slipping away."

Willie reached over and helped him.

"Thanks," Chris said. "OK, next we hook
both the red wires to the little loops on the
bottom of the buzzer." Everyone did that. "Then
all we do is push the switch. Ready?"

Everyone pushed.

Bzzzz bzzzz bz.

"It works!" All three boys yelled at the same
time. Chris bounced out of his chair, stomped
his feet, and jumped around the room while
Willie howled like a wild animal. Sammy kept
his buzzer buzzing.

Chris's little sister, Yoyo, came running into
the kitchen, followed closely by Mrs. Vargas.
She looked worried. "What happened? What's
wrong? Is everything all right?"

"Everything's fine," Chris said, gasping for
breath.

"Listen to this, Mrs. Vargas," Willie said
when he could stop laughing. He touched the
button on his buzzer several times.

Bz bz bz bz bz bz.

"There," he said with a grin, "I just said Hi, isn't this neat?"

Mrs. Vargas touched Chris's buzzer. It worked for her too. *Bzzzzzzzzzz.*

"Well," she said. "It may not be the most pleasant sound, but it sounds better than all that racket I just heard coming from in here!"

"Will you help us a minute, Mom?" Chris asked. "Do you save little plastic tubs—like the kind margarine or butter comes in?"

"Sure," she answered. "I have too many of them. They're on the bottom shelf in the pantry. Help yourself."

Sammy frowned. "What do we need buttertubs for?"

Chris was already digging in the pantry. "You'll see," he said as he backed out. "May I please use a knife to cut holes in the lids, Mom?"

Mrs. Vargas handed him a short, stubby knife and a small breadboard. She watched silently along with Sammy and Willie as Chris cut a rough hole in the top of all three lids.

He brought the containers over to the table and worked as he talked. "Dad said that to make a 'buttertub transmitter' you put the switch through the lid and put the other things

11

inside the box. Oops! I guess I have to take off the switch wires first. Now I'll push it through the lid and hook up the red wires again. There, that was simple!" He held up his finished project for the others to see.

"That's a good idea," Sammy said as he picked up one of the empty buttertubs and began to do the same thing.

Willie grabbed his. "This makes the whole thing easier to carry too!"

Mrs. Vargas smiled as she put the knife away and went back to her sewing machine.

"Can I watch?" Yoyo said hopefully.

Chris moved his buttertub transmitter out of her reach. "Well, OK, but don't touch anything."

For a while the boys played with their buzzers, getting the feel of their switches. Yoyo finally put her hands over her ears and went back to her dolls in the living room.

Chris smiled and said, "Now, let's get down to business." He got pencils and paper for each of them. "Let's take turns sending messages, OK?"

"OK," Willie said, "you go first. Go slow so we can write down the letters we hear. Don't forget what we read about shortcuts." Willie and Sammy picked up their pencils.

".... .. .... — .— .-. ..-" Chris sent.

"OK," Sammy said with a puzzled look. "Here's what I got: 'h-i-h-o-w-r-u.' Huh?"

"Oh, I get it!" Willie exclaimed. "It says: 'Hi, how are you!' Right? This is cool! Now it's my turn."

They soon lost track of time as they sent messages and figured them out. Finally Willie stretched his arms up in the air and wiggled his fingers. "That's enough for now," he said, looking at his watch. "It's almost time for Mom to come get me. Say thanks to your dad for me. This will really help us practice the code. And thanks for the buttertub."

"I'm glad you guys came. Let's do it again tomorrow," Chris said.

"I can't." Willie said. "Grandpa's taking me to the county fair over in the city. We're leaving real early and staying all day. Just Grandpa and me!"

"Well, how about next Monday after school?" Chris asked.

"I'll ask," Willie said, "but I'm pretty sure I can." They both looked at Sammy. He stood still staring into space.

"Wouldn't it be great," he said thoughtfully,

"if we could send this code 'for real' sometime? And really talk to someone?"

On the way home Willie thought about what Sammy had said. *He's right*, Willie decided. *It would be fun to use the Morse code "for real" someday. It would be fun to use it and really help someone.*

2

Rockslide!

"I like this old, winding road much better than the new freeway," Grandpa said. "It takes only a little longer now that most of the traffic is on the freeway. And I really like driving through the hills and trees. This used to be the only way to get to Mill Valley from the city."

Willie relaxed back against the seat of Grandpa's old car. "It's been a super day, hasn't it, Grandpa?"

"That it has, Willie. What did you like best at the county fair?"

"I think I liked the goats best," Willie replied

thoughtfully. "The way they could jump straight up in the air was so funny! That's what I'm going to do when I get to heaven. Jump up and down and run and climb hills—and never get tired! I really liked the cotton candy too."

"I thought food would come into it some-where," Grandpa said with a chuckle. "You ate almost everything at the fair!"

Willie's eyes sparkled as he patted his stomach. "Well, there were lots of things to try. I've never tasted anything called an 'elephant ear' before, have you? I got sugar all over me, but it was yummy." Grandpa smiled and Willie went on. "Another thing I liked was the radio booth. Did you know that Chris and I are learning the Morse code?"

"Well, well! I used to know the Morse code a long time ago. I've forgotten most of it now." Grandpa paused a moment, looking in the rear-view mirror and at the road ahead. "Nobody's around, so how about this?"

He honked the horn one short beep and one long one (. -).

"That's the letter 'A,' " Willie said promptly. "Come on, Grandpa, I know lots of letters. Try something harder."

For a while, Grandpa honked simple words slowly on the horn for Willie.

Finally, Willie grew tired of the game. "How about let's sing?" Willie and Grandpa often sang together when they were in the car.

"Well, let's see. We sang most all the songs you sing in the Shoebox this morning. How about some songs from when I was your age?" Grandpa asked. Before long, Willie was laughing and trying to sing along to Grandpa's old songs.

"Look way down there, Willie," Grandpa said as he drove around a sharp curve. "See that river down at the bottom of the canyon? I'll bet there's a lot of fish down there."

"Yeah, it looks like a zillion miles down though. If my wheelchair started rolling down, I bet I'd break some speed records." Willie glanced into the back seat at his chair.

"If you started down that bank, you'd need a pilot's license, boy," Grandpa joked, "because you'd certainly do some flying."

Willie watched out his window as they drove along. Every new turn took them higher up the mountain. Twenty minutes later, Grandpa pulled the car over and stopped. "Just look at that view, Willie. We're on top of the world. It's all downhill to home now."

Willie pointed to a dark spot in the distance. "Is that Mill Valley? It looks so tiny!"

"That's part of Mill Valley," Grandpa agreed. After a few more minutes of staring, Grandpa put the car in gear and started downhill. "We'll be home in about an hour—just before it gets dark."

Willie grinned. "Good. Because I'll be starved by then."

"Now, why doesn't that surprise me?" Grandpa said laughing. "But we did eat just before we left the fairgrounds, remember?"

Willie just grinned and started reading the road signs out loud. " 'Runaway Truck Ramp, 1/2 Mile.' 'Watch for Falling Rocks.' And look! That one just has a picture of a deer that's flying. Deer don't fly!"

"If you ever saw one bounding across the highway, you'd think they did," Grandpa said.

Willie glanced down the deep canyon on his side of the car and then up toward the bank on Grandpa's side. A movement caught his eye. The bank looked alive! Rocks on it were rolling fast—downhill toward the road!

"Grandpa!" Willie shouted as a brown cloud of dust covered the car. Dirt and rocks whirled around them like a brown blizzard.

"Hang on!" Grandpa shouted. "It's a rockslide!"

A huge rock crashed onto the hood of the car, smashing the windshield. More rocks and clumps of earth fell through the opening onto Willie and Grandpa. Willie gasped for air as the dust and dirt billowed up around him. He heard crashes and bangs as more rocks hit the car. The old car lurched to the right, bumped over the debris on the road, then plunged over the bank.

"Grandpa!" Willie shouted again.

"Hold on, Willie," Grandpa shouted back.

The car shot downward, bumping over bushes and boulders. Rocks and dirt from the road above poured past them like river water. Willie watched, horrified, as they hit a tree stump. For a split second, the car stopped and large rocks rolled past. Then it slid sideways, hit another stump, and spun around to continue its wild slide down the rugged mountainside. Willie was thrown hard against the door, then over toward Grandpa, back and forth, as far as his shoulder belt allowed. Rocks slammed into the side of the car, drowning out all other noises.

"Do something, Grandpa!" Willie shouted.

"Dear God, help us!" Grandpa called, holding his left elbow with his right hand.

"Please, Jesus!" Willie repeated, "help us!"

The car raced on down toward a grove of cedar trees near the bottom of the canyon. As the car entered the trees, the small trees and bushes slowed its speed. Suddenly, the car's front end drove right up over a tall bush and came to rest with the front bumper partway up the side of a big tree. For a minute more, Willie heard only the roar of rocks still rolling down the steep mountainside. Then everything was silent.

Willie coughed and put his hand on his head. "I don't like that ride very much, Grandpa," Willie said in a small, quiet voice. When Grandpa didn't answer, Willie turned to look at him.

Grandpa's head rested on the steering wheel. His eyes were closed. His left arm lay at an odd angle in his lap. His right hand hung limp, almost to the floor.

"Grandpa?" Willie's throat felt tight, and he could hardly breathe. "Grandpa? GRANDPA!"

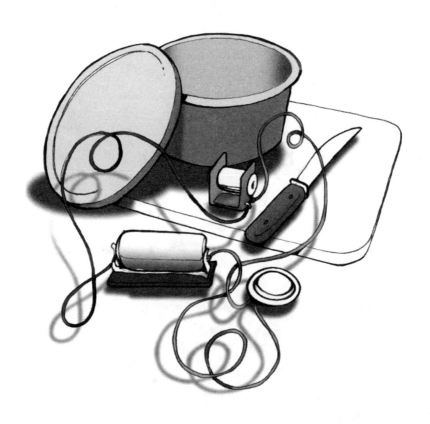

CHAPTER

3

Trapped

"Grandpa, GRANDPA!" Willie shouted. His stomach felt like it had one of the rocks inside it. He shivered. Reaching over, he touched Grandpa's shoulder. Grandpa didn't move.

"GRANDPA," he yelled again. This time he shook Grandpa's shoulder. Grandpa blinked his eyes, then lifted his head and stared at Willie. He blinked again and sat up straight.

"Oh, Willie," he finally said as he really woke up, "are you OK? Are you hurt anywhere?"

Willie moved his arms and felt along his legs. "I'm dirty, but I think I'm OK. How about you?

When you didn't move, I thought something awful had happened to you. I was scared, Grandpa."

"Well, boy," Grandpa said, "I'd say the Lord watched out for us. That was a bad rockslide up there. Where are we anyway? Looks like we're in the middle of a forest."

"We came down a long way," Willie said. "We must be near that little river we saw. Hear it? It doesn't sound so little from down here. What do we do now?"

"Bow your head, Willie," Grandpa said. "The first thing we're going to do is give thanks to God that we're still alive."

"Dear Lord," Grandpa prayed, "thank You for saving our lives. Thank You for keeping the car upright. Please, Lord, help us to stay calm now. We're in a pretty touchy spot, but we know You are here with us. Please, Lord, make somebody miss us soon and guide them to this place. Amen."

"Grandpa, it's going to be dark soon," Willie said nervously, brushing the rocks and dirt off himself. "How's God going to get us home tonight? I don't want to stay here."

"Well, Willie," Grandpa paused a minute to toss several rocks through the broken window beside him. "I suspect we'll be here for a while yet. Why don't we tip our seats back a ways and sing a few songs and watch for the first stars? Then maybe we'll take a little nap. I'm pretty sore and tired."

Not long after the first stars came out, Willie fell soundly asleep.

He woke up with a start when a squirrel scampered across the hood of the old car. The squirrel's little claws clattered on the metal. The sky was bright, and birds were busy. They didn't even seem to notice the black car perched on the side of the tree.

"Hey, Grandpa," Willie said in surprise, "we've been here all night! Mom and Dad must really be worried about us. And I'm starving!"

"Willie," Grandpa began, "you and I and the Lord have some problems to face. You see, Willie, we'll have to wait to be found. I didn't mention it last night, but one of those big boulders must have smashed into my side of the car. My foot's caught. It doesn't feel like it's hurt much, but I can't get it loose. Besides, I wouldn't want to leave you here alone, and I'm sure I couldn't carry you back up that steep hill to the road."

Willie hardly knew what to say. He didn't

really want to stay in the car alone, but how else could they get help? "I'd be OK, Grandpa. Are you sure you can't get your foot loose?"

Grandpa shook his head. "I tried for a good long while before you woke up. I'm sure. We're here to stay until help arrives. Now, how about breakfast?"

Willie wondered if his grandpa was thinking right. "Breakfast? That's what they're having at home now."

Grandpa smiled. "Then let's have some too. Remember that box of graham crackers we put in the back seat? I think I can reach it. How about Graham crackers for breakfast?"

It was Willie's turn to smile. "That would be great! And we have the apples we didn't eat at lunch yesterday." He reached down for the crumpled bag on the floor near his feet and dumped the two apples on the seat beside him. "And we still have water in our bottles."

"Why, boy," Grandpa said, "we'll have a breakfast fit for a king!"

While they ate, Willie thought to himself, *If only I had two good legs, I could go up to the road and get help. But I'd never get anywhere in my chair!*

"What's the matter?" Grandpa asked. "Why so quiet all of a sudden?"

"Just thinking," Willie answered, his voice getting higher as he spoke. "I wish I could go for help, Grandpa. I can't do anything but just sit here."

"What's your memory verse for this week?" Grandpa asked abruptly.

" 'The angel of the Lord encamps around those who fear him, and he delivers them,' Psalm 34:7," Willie recited. After a small hesitation, he realized what Grandpa was getting at. "Oh yeah! The angels are here, aren't they?"

"Well, this looks like a pretty good place to do some 'angel camping' to me." Grandpa smiled as he looked out at the dark-green trees and the yellow wildflowers. He eased himself into a more comfortable position. Willie noticed that Grandpa was holding his left arm carefully with his right hand.

"What's the matter with your arm?" he asked. "Does it hurt?"

"Yes, it hurts a little," Grandpa replied. "I think it may be broken." For a second, Grandpa's eyes showed a lot of pain and sadness. Then he turned back to Willie and smiled a little smile.

"You're a smart boy," he said. "You can see the fix we're in. But Jesus knows where we are and what we can do to help ourselves. Our part's to figure out what we can do. We'll leave Him to bring help."

"But what will we do?" Willie asked as he munched on another Graham cracker. "I can't walk, and your foot is stuck. So what can we do?"

"Well, the first thing you can do is to take it easy on those crackers!" Grandpa said with a grin. "We might want to eat again today!"

Willie grinned back and closed the box. Then he took a drink from his water bottle. "I guess I shouldn't drink very much water either. I know what let's do! Let's say all the Bible verses we can remember. We'll take turns and see who can keep going the longest!"

"Are you thinking," Grandpa asked, giving him a playful poke, "that maybe those angels who are 'camping around' us will be impressed and 'deliver' us?"

Willie grinned again. " 'The Lord is my shepherd,' " he began. " 'I will not want. He makes me lie down in green pastures . . . ' "

For a long time they recited verses, searching their memories for more.

"'. . . For He shall give His angels charge over you,'" Grandpa quoted, "'to keep you in all your ways.'"

"Grandpa!" shouted Willie suddenly. "I've got it!"

Grandpa was puzzled. "Got what?"

"I know what to do to help us!" Willie bounced in his seat. "Jesus must have put the idea into my mind."

"What are you talking about?" Grandpa asked.

Willie smiled. "You'll see," he said, opening the glove compartment. As he pulled out the papers and maps, he said, "Now, if I can just find what I need."

4

S.O.S.

"I didn't know that much stuff could fit in there," Grandpa said as he watched the pile in Willie's lap growing higher. "What are you looking for?"

Willie sighed. "Oh, Grandpa, I was so sure Jesus had given me a good idea—but you don't have a flashlight!" Willie's voice sounded almost like a wail.

"Sure, I have a flashlight. It's right here under the dash." With some effort, Grandpa reached under the dashboard and brought out the large green flashlight held there by a magnet.

"Now, what do you want this for?" Grandpa asked. "It's daylight out."

"But it won't be daylight tonight!" Willie said, happily pushing the 'flash' button on the flashlight. "Did you forget, Grandpa? We know the Morse code!"

Grandpa slowly stroked his chin and said, "Yes, I guess I did. You're right; Jesus did give you a good idea. I've been worrying about our headlights facing away from the road. And here you thought of the flashlight! Good thinking! I thought of using the horn to get someone's attention. But I tried it, and it doesn't work."

Willie held up his hand. "Listen, Grandpa," he said in a whisper. "Hear that?"

Off in the distance, they could hear the sound of a motor.

"One thing for sure," Grandpa said, "they won't be driving on that road above. That landslide must have made a huge mess of the road."

During the afternoon, Willie and Grandpa talked quietly. Both were waiting for the sun to go down so they could send light signals. Two more times they heard motors in the distance. Willie noticed one motor getting louder. He and Grandpa looked at each other as the sound became a roar. Grandpa's eyebrows went up; his eyes were wide open.

Willie's heart beat a little faster. Through the trees he cold see a small plane coming toward them. His hands curled into fists, his muscles tightened. *Please, Jesus*, he prayed, *make them see us.*

The plane came nearer. It passed directly over the car. Then he and Grandpa watched it disappear. Willie had to fight to keep from crying.

Finally Grandpa spoke again. "Say, did you see a big safety pin in that glove compartment? I sure could use one." Willie noticed that Grandpa still cradled his left arm.

"I don't remember," Willie said as he opened it up and began to pull the paper and maps out again.

"Here's one," he said, holding it out to Grandpa. "What are you going to do with it?"

"You'll have to do it for me," Grandpa said. "Can you manage to pin the cuff of my sleeve to my shirt pocket? Pin it here, where I'm holding it. It'll make sort of a sling; then my arm won't hurt so much. Ah-h-h, that's much better."

Dear Jesus, Willie prayed in his thoughts, *we do need to be rescued. I'll send the signals when it gets dark. Won't you please send someone to see them?*

Willie picked up his water bottle and took a sip. Grandpa looked at him with concern. "Willie," Grandpa said slowly, "better take it easy on the water. It's all we've got. We might need some for tomorrow—if—if no one comes."

"If only I could climb down out of this car and out of the tree," Willie said, "I could get us some water. It's not far. I can hear the river. Oh, Grandpa, if only I could walk."

"Well, boy," Grandpa said, "your legs may not work, but your brain sure does. And with Jesus helping, there'll be no stopping you. Now, don't you worry. We just need to be careful with our food and water—just in case."

About the time the first stars came out, Willie began to feel a sense of excitement. *What message should I send?* he asked himself. *Oh yeah, S-O-S. That's the distress signal. Let's see. Three dots, three dashes, three dots. Three short flashes, three long flashes, three short flashes. That won't be too hard.*

"Well, it looks like it's dark enough now, don't you think?" Grandpa said at last. "Let's pray first."

"OK," Willie said, "I'll do it. Dear Jesus, we're going to do our part now. Will you please send someone to look this way and find us? Thank You for being here with us. Amen."

"Amen," Grandpa added. Then he reached awkwardly to the left side of the dashboard with his right hand and turned on the car lights. Only one light came on. It lighted up the tree trunk right in front of them, making eerie shadows in the branches.

Willie held the flashlight out the window, pointing it up the hill behind them. His thumb on the flasher button, he sent:

"... — ... ... — ..."

He flashed the SOS about twenty times. *Please, Jesus,* he prayed silently, *let someone see it. Please, Jesus.*

He strained his ears to hear sounds, any sounds that might mean "rescue." Once he thought he heard a motor. After a brief rest for his thumb, he started sending the message again.

Then he heard a car horn. It sounded far away, but it kept up. Suddenly Willie grabbed for the pencil and paper in the glove compartment. "R-U," he wrote. The horn stopped a moment. Willie stared at the paper. He soon realized he had heard only the last part of the message.

When it began again, Willie was ready to copy all the sounds. His hand shook, and his breath came in short puffs as he heard:

".— .... — .-. ..-"

And he copied, "W-H-O–R-U"

5

The Search Begins

Earlier that morning back in Mill Valley, Chris dialed the telephone number for Willie's house. "Hello, Mrs. Taylor. May I speak to Willie?" he asked. "Sammy and I are going to practice the Morse code this afternoon, and we wanted him to come too."

"Oh, Chris," Mrs. Taylor began. She paused to swallow a lump in her throat. "He isn't here. You may as well know that Willie and Grandpa didn't come home last night. We are very worried about them."

"Where are they?" he asked.

"We don't know," she said, swallowing again. "They haven't phoned. I'm afraid something happened to them. Mr. Taylor called the police and, so far, they have no reports of an accident involving an old black car like Willie's grandpa drives."

Chris was concerned for his friend. "Can I do anything?"

"You can pray, Chris," Mrs. Taylor said promptly. "You and the other Shoebox kids could pray for them. Pray that they're safe—and—and that they'll be found soon."

"We sure will, Mrs. Taylor," Chris said. "I'll call Mrs. Shue. She'll want to be praying for Willie too."

Chris made several phone calls right away, and within thirty minutes all of the Shoebox kids were at the church. Mrs. Shue arrived five minutes later.

"Well, kids," she said as she unlocked the big front door and led the way to the Shoebox, "this really is something to worry about. But we know that Jesus sends His angels to watch over us. And we know that He loves Willie and his grandpa even more than we do."

Maria spoke first. "I think we should ask

Jesus to have someone find them real soon—like today—or tonight."

Sammy had been sitting quietly. Now he spoke up. "Let's get in a circle and start praying, OK?"

Each of them prayed earnestly for Willie and his grandpa, asking Jesus to protect them and bring them home safely.

"Now," DeeDee said, when they were ready to leave, "Call me if you hear anything, Chris. Then I'll call you, Jenny, and you can call Sammy."

"I'm going home with Chris for a while," Sammy told her.

After the goodbyes, Chris and Sammy stood around awkwardly. They felt they should be doing something to find Willie, but they didn't know where to begin or what to do. "Let's go practice the code," Chris finally said.

The boys were working hard on their buzzers when the doorbell rang. "Chris," Maria called, "it's Ryan."

"We're in the kitchen, Ryan," Chris called. Ryan lived next door, and he was one of Chris's best friends. He visited the Shoebox once in a while, so he knew Sammy.

Maria shrugged. "If you can stand the noise, go on in," she said.

Ryan stood in the kitchen doorway for a moment then put his hands over his ears. "What are you guys doing? Playing with plastic pails? Come on, let's go play baseball or something."

Chris and Sammy looked at each other. They didn't quite know what to say. "Willie is missing," Chris finally blurted out. He explained what they knew. "And these are buttertub transmitters. We're learning Morse code."

Ryan stared closely at the buttertubs then pushed the buzzer on Chris's. "I still say it's boring. Come on! Let's go do something."

"No way," Chris answered. "I want to learn Morse code. Besides, we're waiting to hear about Willie. Willie's mom is going to call here if she finds out where they are."

Ryan nodded. "I understand that. But I don't understand this code stuff. I'd rather go out and do something to help find them. See you later."

After Ryan left, Sammy asked, "I'd rather go out and do something too. But what could we do?"

Just then, Mr. Vargas walked into the kitchen. "Hi, Dad!" Chris exclaimed. "Did you hear about

Willie and his grandpa? Wait a minute—what are you doing home in the middle of the day?"

"Your mom called me at work to tell me about Willie," he said. "I knew you'd be worried, so I came home to see what we could do."

"Can we do something?" Sammy asked, jumping up.

"Well, how would you boys like to go help in the search?" Mr. Vargas asked.

"Can we?" both boys shouted at once.

"Well," he answered, "you guys make some sandwiches in case we miss supper, and I'll call Sammy's parents for permission to go with us. Maria will probably want to go too."

Before long, the boys were waiting in the back seat of the car along with their bag of sandwiches. "Come on, come on, come on," Chris muttered as they waited. Finally, his dad came out. While they waited for Maria, Mr. Vargas told the boys about the searching efforts already being done.

"Willie's dad has been searching along the highway today. The State Police and the county sheriff have also been notified and are keeping an eye out for them. Even small plane owners at the Mill Valley airport have been asked to help."

"Wow!" Chris said. "Somebody should find them pretty soon with all those people looking."

"Oh, that's not all," Mr. Vargas said. "Mr. and Mrs. Shue are going out to search this afternoon also. I think DeeDee and Jenny are going with them. They'll go on some of the back roads in the hills, just in case Willie and his grandpa decided to go roaming the hills and their car broke down."

"Well, let's go!" Chris urged. He leaned out the window and shouted, "Maria! Hurry up! Let's go!"

As they backed down the driveway, Chris noticed a small boxy-looking black thing with push-buttons on it in the front seat. "What's that?" he asked.

"A CB radio," Mr. Vargas replied. "The sheriff's department is supplying them to the searchers. We need to stay in contact with each other. If one of us finds them, we need to let the other searchers know."

"Great idea," Chris said.

"Shouldn't we pray before we go?" Sammy quietly suggested.

"Good thinking," Mr. Vargas said. He pulled over to the side of the road. "Would you like to pray for us, Sammy?"

Sammy bowed his head and prayed for Willie and his grandpa and asked Jesus to direct the searchers.

As they drove toward the edge of town, Maria asked, "Where are we going, Dad? This road doesn't go to the freeway."

"No," Mr. Vargas replied, "we're going on an old road, one that isn't used much anymore. It used to be the only road between Mill Valley and the city. I don't think they'd come that way, but we want to check just in case."

6

A Light in the Night

For several hours, Mr. Vargas drove up the old highway, turning down side roads for a mile or two then returning to the main road. Sometimes he stopped so Chris, Sammy, and Maria could get out and look down into deep canyons, hoping for a sign of a small black car. Finally, Mr. Vargas pulled off the road and parked in a wide area where people stopped to enjoy the view.

"Anybody hungry?" he asked.

"Not really, Dad," Chris said in a subdued voice. "I don't feel much like eating."

"It's going to get dark soon," Maria said. "Won't we have to go home? We can't see anything anyway."

"You never know what you'll see," Mr. Vargas said. "Let's get out and stretch our legs and eat the sandwiches. It's already after seven. And lunch was a long time ago."

"Will we go up this road a little farther before we go home, Mr. Vargas?" Sammy asked. "I'd really like to."

"We sure will," Mr. Vargas replied. "We won't quit until we're convinced they aren't on this road. I told your folks to expect us to be late. Now, while you kids eat, I'm going to contact the other searchers and see if there's any news."

While Chris, Sammy, and Maria gathered around a picnic table to eat, Mr. Vargas sat in the car and talked on the CB radio. Soon he joined them. "They say 'No news is good news,'" he said. "No one has seen anything that even looked like that old black car."

"Dad, can we go on now?" Chris asked softly. "It's getting dark, and I want to keep looking as long as we can."

"Sure, son," Mr. Vargas said, giving Chris a quick hug. "I'm concerned too. I'll drive, you look, and we'll all pray." Then he called to the others, "Let's go! Be sure to bring all the trash from your food. We don't want to leave anything behind."

Mr. Vargas drove slowly on the old winding road. The kids shouted for him to stop often, thinking they saw something important. After each false alarm, they got back into the car a little more discouraged.

Maria, who was in the front seat, suddenly yelled, "Watch out, Dad!"

Mr. Vargas slammed on the brakes just in time to keep from hitting some large rocks in the road. The kids jumped out of the car to explore.

"Look!" Sammy shouted. "Look at all the rocks and dirt on the road."

"And look at those two big boulders!" Maria added. "One things for sure, nobody could get through this road!"

"That's one big landslide," Mr. Vargas agreed as he joined them. "Maria, I'm glad you were helping me watch the road. With these curves and the darkness, it's impossible to see very far ahead."

"Mr. Vargas?" Sammy said in a strange voice.

"Yes, Sammy?"

"Do you think there would be a farmhouse down there?" Sammy was looking over the side of the road, down into the deep canyon. "There's something way down there that looks sort of lighted up. That seems funny."

"Dad!" Chris yelled as he joined Sammy. "There's another light! Look? You can barely make it out. Wait a minute—dot-dot-dot, dash-dash-dash, dot-dot-dot! Dad, someone is signaling for help. That's S-O-S!"

"Maybe it's Willie!" Sammy said. His voice was tense.

"WILLIE," Sammy said. "It's got to be Willie! WILLIE! WILLIE!" He jumped up and down as he hollered.

"Quick, Chris," Mr. Vargas ordered, "get the flashlight and signal back. If it isn't Willie, it's someone else who needs help."

Chris hurried back with the flashlight and began to flash it randomly. "What shall I say?" he asked.

"Find out if it's Willie!" Maria cried.

Chris sent a message several times, but the light below just kept signaling the same S-O-S call.

"Maybe," Sammy said, "whoever it is can't

see your light."

"Why don't we try the horn?" Maria suggested.

"In the meantime," Mr. Vargas said, "I'll get on the radio and let the sheriff know that somebody needs help."

Chris reached into the car to get a tablet and a pencil. "Here, Sammy," he said. "I'll do the sending, and you write down the signals—if we get any back. Maria, come hold the flashlight for Sammy. Then we can figure it out together. Ryan should see us now! Maybe he wouldn't think the Morse code was such a waste of time."

Chris stood by the open car door and pushed on the horn. *Honk. Honk-honk.*

"What are you saying?" Maria asked as Chris kept pushing the horn.

"What you said, Sis," Chris replied. "I'm simply asking who's down there. Sure wish I'd studied the punctuation marks though. I hope they know I'm asking a question, even with no question mark."

Chris continued to repeat his message: "Who are you-who are you-who are you."

Then the S-O-S from down in the canyon stopped.

"Dad?" Chris said. Everyone could hear the worry in Chris's voice.

"Be patient, Chris," he said. "If that is Willie down there, he doesn't know the code very well yet."

"Oh, Dad, it's just got to be Willie!"

"Look!" Dad said in reply, pointing to a pinpoint of light in the darkness far below. "There's your answer coming!"

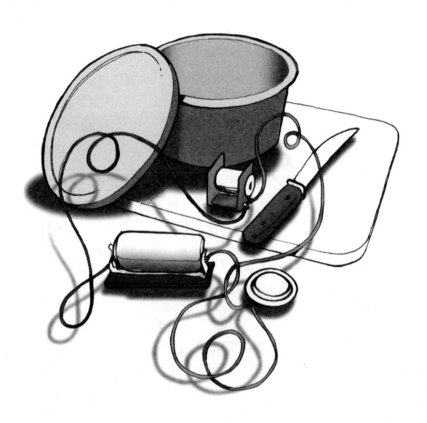

7

Morse Code Rescue

Chris and Sammy watched the flashing light carefully.

"._"

"Was that a letter?" Chris asked. "What letter was it?"

"I think it was a 'W,'" Sammy said. The light kept flashing.

"..-"

"I know that one," Chris said. "That's an 'I.'" He kept watching the light.

".-.. .-.."

"What was that?" Sammy asked. "No letter

code is that long. Wait a minute! That was two letters! Two 'Ws!" The light kept flashing.

"..- ."

"It's Willie!" Chris and Sammy shouted together.

Far down below, inside the car, Willie and Grandpa sat waiting silently. Willie hardly dared to breathe. They listened, not wanting to miss a single horn honk. *What's happening up there?* Willie wondered. *Who is it? Why don't they answer me?*

When the sounds came, Willie was ready. He wrote down a letter for each sound he heard. His grin spread from one ear to the other, but the lump in his throat grew so big he couldn't speak for a moment.

"Well, Willie?" Grandpa said anxiously. "Who is it? What did they say? I didn't get all of it."

"It's Chris," he replied in a small voice. "It's Chris!" he repeated a little louder. "Oh, Grandpa, it's Chris!" He threw his arms around as much of Grandpa as he could reach and hugged him.

"Better answer him," Grandpa suggested.

Willie wrote down the words he wanted to send. Then carefully he flashed each letter, trying to keep the light steady. It was hard not to bounce up and down and wave his arms.

"I told him to take us home," Willie said when he finished. "How long do you think it'll take them to get us out of here?"

"Chris and his dad won't be able to come get us," Grandpa replied. "It will probably be the sheriff or the forestry service. Remember—we didn't see any roads down here. We made our own road down the mountain. It would be dangerous for whoever's up there with Chris to come down the way we—"

Willie interrupted. "Listen, Grandpa! Hear that?" He began to copy what he heard.

"-L-P-C-O-M-I-N-G-S-O-O-N"

Willie looked at his tablet with a frown as he tried to figure out the message. "It must say 'help coming soon.' Yes, that's what it means. Great! We'll be out of here soon!"

"I hope so, boy," Grandpa said slowly. "I hope so."

"Is your arm hurting a lot?" Willie asked.

"M-hm." Then after a moment, Grandpa added, "Now, comes the hard part: waiting for the rescue.

"But Chris said that help is coming soon!"

Willie almost wailed.

"Be patient," Grandpa said. "For right now, it's enough to know that Jesus sent someone to see our signals. Help will come."

After what seemed like hours, Willie heard a low roar in the distance. The sound grew louder and louder. "What is it, Grandpa?" Willie shouted above the noise.

"Sounds like a helicopter," Grandpa yelled back.

A bright light flashed down from the darkness above, lighting up the trees. It moved in slow circles toward the car. Then suddenly the light flooded through the broken windows of the car.

A deep voice called out through a loudspeaker somewhere above the light. "Willie Taylor, wave your hand if you are both OK. Wave your hand if you are both OK."

Willie stuck his arm out the window and waved frantically.

The voice boomed again. "Can you make it until morning? Wave your hand for 'Yes.' "

Willie was slower at putting out his hand this time, and he waved very slowly.

"Good! We will be back for you," the voice

boomed. "We will be back."

With that, the light vanished and the helicopter roared away.

8

Angel in a Red Hat

In the black stillness that followed, neither Grandpa nor Willie spoke. Willie thought about the voice from above.

"Grandpa," he said softly several minutes later. "Do you think they'll come back soon?"

"It's hard to say," Grandpa said. "Probably not till morning—like the man said."

"I wonder if that's what Jesus' voice sounds like," Willie said thoughtfully. "When that voice called my name, I thought for just a minute that Jesus had come to help us."

"Don't you think—He did?" Grandpa spoke

slowly, like it hurt to talk. "He often uses—people to do his work—you know. Other people—and His angels."

Willie noticed that Grandpa's voice sounded weak and tired. *Dear Jesus,* he prayed silently, *thank You for sending the helicopter and your angels.* But, *Jesus, something's wrong with Grandpa. We need to go home. Please have your angels protect us for one more night. And please, please send people to get . . .*

Willie fell asleep.

When his eyes opened again, Willie felt confused. Something was different, but what?

A beautiful sunrise made the sky all pink and blue. Squirrels played on the hood of the car again. Birds sang on branches just above it. The cedar trees smelled tangy. The small river still made its noisy way over the rocks. But what was different?

He heard voices. Voices? Voices!

"Grandpa!" Willie exclaimed. "I hear voices!"

Grandpa looked over at Willie and smiled weakly. "Thank You, Lord," he said. Then he closed his eyes again.

"Willie! Willie Taylor!" Several voices were shouting Willie's name.

"I'm here!" Willie called back. "We're right here!"

"Hang on, buddy. We're coming!" Willie could hear the sounds of people tramping through the brush and trees.

Then the trees seemed to part, and four men appeared. One had a stretcher strapped on his back; two others had packs on. The fourth man wore a red baseball cap and had a coil of rope over his shoulder.

"Hey, buddy! How ya' doing?" the man in the red hat said. He seemed to be the leader.

"What're you doing sitting up in that tree," another man joked, while a third man talked into a radio.

Willie didn't know whether he was going to laugh or cry for a second.

"Are you angels?" he asked.

"Angels?" the man in the red hat laughed. "Shucks, buddy, we're no angles!"

"But we do help them out now and then," the man with the stretcher spoke up.

He and one of the other men had gone around to Grandpa's side of the car. "Mr. Taylor? Mr. Taylor, how are you feeling?"

Grandpa just smiled and nodded his head.

"Please help Grandpa first," Willie begged. "He hurts a lot, I think."

While the other men worked to free Grandpa, the man with the red hat spoke to Willie.

"I'm Joe Mason," he said as he reached up and pulled the car door open. Then he held up a canteen. "Want a drink?"

"Yeah, thanks," Willie said, reaching for the canteen. He took three big gulps, then handed it back.

"Well, now," Mr. Mason said, "are you ready to get out of there?"

"Yes, sir!" Willie responded.

Mr. Mason stepped onto a low branch so he was on a level with Willie. He put his finger on Willie's wrist to feel his heartbeat.

"Do you hurt anywhere? I don't see any blood, but you sure are dirty!" he said with a chuckle. "Did you bring half the mountain down inside the car?"

Then he put his left hand on Willie's right knee, and with the other hand he felt along Willie's leg and foot. He did the same with Willie's left leg.

"Now look at me," Mr. Mason said. He grabbed Willie by the chin and turned his head. He looked in each of Willie's eyes and in both ears.

"Well, buddy," he said at last. "You look in pretty good shape. Just a few bruises here and there. What kind of diet you been on?"

"Graham crackers!" Willie said with a grin. "Water and Graham crackers. Can we go home now, please?"

"That's exactly what we're going to do. Your folks are pretty anxious to see you," Mr. Mason replied as he looked through the car to the men helping Grandpa. "How are you guys doing, Dave?"

"We just got his leg free, Joe," Dave, the man who had carried the stretcher replied. Then he spoke gently to Grandpa. "We're going to put a splint on your arm now, Mr. Taylor. You'll be more comfortable then."

"Let's go, buddy," Mr. Mason said, reaching into the car. He slid one long arm under Willie's legs and another behind his back. "Put your arm around my neck, OK?" He lifted Willie easily and stepped off the low branch onto the ground.

"Grandpa?" Willie called to his grandfather, but he got no answer. He turned to Mr. Mason. "What's going to happen to Grandpa?"

"My men will take good care of him," Mr. Mason said as he and Willie neared the river. "They'll carry him out on a stretcher."

Mr. Mason stopped and turned around. "Do you want to see some friends of yours?" he said. He tilted his eyes and chin to point Willie's attention up the mountainside—way, way up the mountainside. Willie could just barely see tiny people looking over the bank, watching the rescue down below.

"Chris?" Willie asked. "Is that Chris? He answered my S-O-S."

"Yeah, I hear you're pretty good with the Morse code on the flashlight!" Mr. Mason joked as he balanced on a log and crossed the river.

Willie noticed a big, square four-wheel-drive truck with the word "Sheriff" in gold letters on the side. "There's a road here?" he asked.

"Well, sort of a road," Mr. Mason replied. "It's an old logging road. Hasn't been used for years. But you can drive down it if you have to. And it brought us to you."

"Now I'm going to lay you down and strap you to this bed," he continued as he stepped up into the back of the truck. "Don't worry. This is just standard procedure. Your folks will meet us at the hospital. A doctor will check you over and decide if you can go home or whether you need to stay awhile."

As Mr. Mason talked, Willie noticed the other men coming along the trail. Two of them carried Grandpa strapped on the stretcher. The last man carried Willie's wheelchair.

"With just a little repair, I think this'll work fine," he said as he put it in the truck.

Then the men gently lifted Grandpa's stretcher into the truck. Willie watched wide-eyed.

"Are you OK, Grandpa?" He knew his voice sounded scared.

Grandpa wiggled his fingers in a tiny wave. "He's worn out," the one called Dave said, "but he'll feel better by tomorrow."

"Hey, Mr. Taylor," Mr. Mason's voice boomed cheerfully. "Didn't that Graham-cracker diet agree with you?"

Grandpa just smiled then closed his eyes.

As the truck began to bump slowly along the old road, Dave sat down by Willie and patted his arm. "You've been a brave kid," he said. "How did you happen to know the Morse code? Not many people use it anymore."

All the way back to Mill Valley, Willie talked with Dave. He told Dave about practicing the code, about the landslide, and about praying to be rescued.

"You know," Dave said, "I think it's one of God's miracles that you and your grandpa are alive after all you've been through. That was quite a landslide—and a rough trip down the mountain. Angels helped you. I'm certain of it."

At long last, Willie could tell they were in town, because the truck was on a smooth road and because he could hear a lot of cars.

Joe Mason had been leaning over Grandpa doing things to him for most of the trip. He talked on a telephone several times, listening and nodding his head. Once he took out a big needle and gave Grandpa a shot. Willie watched while he talked to Dave.

Finally he burst out, "Are you sure Grandpa is really OK? He looks so white!" Willie's eyes were open wide, and he felt a big lump in his throat as big as a golf ball.

"He doesn't move! Is Grandpa going to die? Is he?"

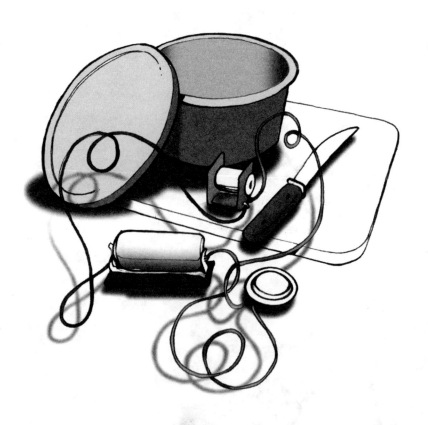

CHAPTER

9

Home at Last

Dave opened his mouth to reply, but just then the truck stopped, and the back doors were thrown open. A lady in a white coat reached in to help Dave get Willie's stretcher out of the truck.

"Hi, Willie," she said. "I'm Dr. Matthews. How are you doing?"

"OK," Willie answered. "But what about my grandpa?"

She looked over at Dave. "It looks as if he'll be OK too."

Willie felt a little better. But he was con-

73

fused. "How did you know my name?" he asked the doctor.

"Why, don't you know? You're famous!" she answered. "I heard about the search for you and your grandpa on the radio yesterday. Everyone's been looking for you."

Willie smiled. As he raised his head, he saw his mom and dad standing on the other side of the glass hospital doors. Dad had an arm around Mom, and she was wiping her eyes with a big white handkerchief.

After that, things got blurry for Willie. Bright lights in his eyes; white coats; Mom with a watery smile; medicine smells; a hard, narrow bed with a white paper sheet that crackled when he moved.

Three hours later, a nurse wheeled Willie out to the car.

"But—where's Grandpa?" Willie craned his neck to look behind him. "We have to wait for Grandpa!"

"Grandpa won't be coming home today," Dad said as he lifted Willie into the car. "He has to stay so the doctors can be sure he'll be OK. He'll be home in a day or two."

"Are you sure he'll be OK? He won't die or

anything, will he?"

"Hey, where did you get that idea?" Dad replied as he slid behind the steering wheel. "Grandpa will be fine. But you didn't eat very well the last few days. And you didn't have much water. You're young and strong, but Grandpa's not. And remember, he has a broken arm too."

Willie was too tired to think anymore. So he laid his head back against the seat and closed his eyes. When he woke up, the car was in the driveway at his house, and something was licking his face. He reached up and felt a wiggly, furry body.

"Coco!" he exclaimed, hugging his brown and white dog.

Later, after a big lunch, Willie snuggled down in bed with a smile on his face and Coco at his feet. And just before he fell asleep, he whispered, "Thank You for getting us rescued, Jesus. Thanks a lot."

The next thing Willie knew, his mother's voice was calling. "Hey, Sleepyhead," Mom said cheerfully. "Are you going to sleep all day today too?"

"Huh?" Willie opened one eye. It was daylight. "What do you mean? Is it tomorrow?"

"Yes, it's tomorrow." Mom laughed. "Chris and Sammy called. They're coming over soon. So how about a bath and some breakfast?"

When Chris and Sammy arrived, they wanted to hear all about the accident and what it was like down in the canyon. But Willie had questions of his own.

"How did you find us?" he asked, looking at Chris. So Chris told about the search and how he and Sammy had looked and looked for him. "You were there, too, Sammy?" Willie was surprised.

"Of course he was there," Chris said. Sammy just smiled. "Who do you think wrote down your messages? I couldn't do everything . . ."

Willie interrupted. "But how did you get back so early the next morning?"

"We never left," Sammy spoke softly.

"What! You stayed all night?"

"Well," Chris replied, "first Dad wanted to stay until the helicopter found you. He was talking on the radio to the pilot."

Sammy continued the story. "And we just couldn't go home and leave you down there. We just couldn't."

"So we stayed," Chris said, "and we prayed for you."

Sammy spoke up again. "Do you remember how we wondered if we could ever do anything 'real' with the Morse code?"

"Yeah," Willie said thoughtfully, "I've been thinking a lot about that."

Soon the boys left, promising to come back in a few days, when Willie had caught up on his sleep and felt stronger.

They came again two days later, bringing their buttertub transmitters. For an hour, they practiced the Morse code at the Taylor's kitchen table.

"I wonder what time it is," Sammy said, stretching his arms in the air. "Seems like—a— you know—."

"Hold your horses," Chris said, grinning.

"What are you guys talking about?" Willie asked.

Just then, Willie's mom walked in with a puzzled look on her face.

"What's the matter, Mom?" Willie asked.

"I don't *think* anything is wrong," she replied slowly, "but someone from the Sheriff's Department just called to say they were on their way here."

CHAPTER

Surprise!

"The Sheriff's Department? What do they want?" Willie asked. As he spoke, the front door opened. "Dad! How come you're home so early?"

Dad winked at Mom and set his briefcase down. "Can't a man come to his own home in the middle of the day?" he asked, smiling.

Mom just looked at Dad, her eyebrows raised.

The doorbell rang. Dad opened the door and made a funny little bow as the rest of the Shoebox kids bounded into the living room, followed by Mrs. Shue. Willie looked quickly at Chris and Sammy. They were whispering to

81

6—R.R.

each other; then they grinned at Willie.

"Welcome home!" everyone shouted. Then they all talked at once, each one trying to be heard above the others. Coco ran in circles, yapping.

Then a voice boomed above them all. "Can we join the party?"

For one instant, everyone was silent, staring at the two big men in sheriff's uniforms. A smaller man dressed in jeans was behind them. Then Willie let out a squeal. "Mr. Mason! Dave! Wow!" Then he turned to his Shoebox friends and said proudly, "These are the men who rescued Grandpa and me. And, Mr. Mason, Chris and Sammy are the ones who found me," he said, pointing them out.

"I didn't recognize you at first, Mr. Mason," Willie added. "Not without your red baseball cap."

"Hey, buddy," he replied, "I can't wear my red cap with my dress uniform. And this visit is official business." As he spoke, he glanced around at all the Shoebox kids, now sitting quietly, looking up expectantly. "Mr. Taylor thought that all of you might like to be here for this. Oh, and this man" he added, nodding toward the man in jeans who was holding a camera, "is a reporter from the Mill Valley newspaper."

"But—why?" Willie's mom asked. "I'm still confused."

"You'll see," his dad said quietly, with a smile.

Then Mr. Mason and Dave stood side-by-side, straight and tall, in front of Willie. They looked very important. The reporter adjusted his camera. Mr. Mason held up a crisp official-looking piece of white paper.

"Willie Taylor," he said in his big, deep voice, "because of your actions that resulted in you and your grandfather being found and rescued, the Mill County Sheriff's Department awards you this Certificate of Bravery." He handed the certificate to Willie as the camera flashed and the kids cheered.

Willie beamed with pleasure. He felt a warm glow inside. He noticed his mom wiping a tear off her cheek.

After the men left, the kids sat quietly talking for a while. Then Mrs. Shue spoke up. "Willie, was it scary down there in the canyon?"

"Yeah," Willie shuddered, remembering. "I knew angels were there, but it was scary—especially the first night. You know," he continued, "I fussed because I couldn't walk and go for help. I prayed and I wanted God to make a miracle." He paused before speaking again. "I think I understand things better now. I need to work on learning everything I can, and Jesus will tell me how to use what I learn."

Chris laughed and said, "When we were practicing the code, I never thought we'd use it to get you rescued."

"That's it," Willie replied. "See, we can trust Jesus to take care of us and to show us how to use what we know to help others—and ourselves," he added with a grin.

"If you've learned that, Willie," Mrs. Shue said, "You've learned something many adults don't know yet."

Dad was hanging up the phone as Mrs. Shue finished speaking.

"Good news, Willie! I can bring Grandpa home in time for supper tonight!"

Again the kids cheered.

Dad picked up his briefcase and held up his hand for silence.

"Willie Taylor," he said in a deep voice. The kids laughed at his imitation of Mr. Mason.

"Willie Taylor," he repeated, sounding more

like himself, "because of your bravery and quick thinking, your mother and I would like to present you with something to make the Morse code more fun for you to practice."

He reached into his briefcase and took out a small package. He handed it to Willie.

"We know you were hoping for the Morse code computer program next Christmas, but we decided you could use it now."

"Oh, cool!" Willie exclaimed. He tore open the wrapping and held up the box. "I don't know what Jesus will use me for next, but I'll be ready."

How to Make a "Buttertub" Transmitter

Things to buy: 1—Momentary Push-Button Soft-Feel Switch
1— 1.5 to 3 VDC Mini Buzzer
1—Battery Holder for AA or AAA batteries
Batteries to fit the Holder

Recycle: 1—clean butter or margarine container with a lid
(A one-pound container or smaller is best.)

Directions: 1. Get a grown-up to help you cut a hole in the lid.
About one-half inch hole should be big enough.*
2. Unscrew the thin metal nut from the switch.

Push the switch through the hole and screw the nut back on.
This will hold it tightly in place. (Make sure the red button is on the *outside* of the lid.)

3. Notice that both the battery holder and the buzzer have two wires, one black and one red.

4. Tape, twist, or hook the black wires to each other. Make sure the bare wires are touching.

5. Hook one red wire to each of the little holes in the metal tabs on the bottom of the switch.

6. Gently lower the lid (and all the things connected to it) over the buttertub and seal

the lid.

7. Push the buzzer and have fun!

* I used an old paper punch to make a few extra holes in the lid so I could hear the sound better.

THE MORSE CODE

A	. –	N	– .
B	– . . .	O	– – –
C	– . – .	P	. – – .
D	– . .	Q	– – . –
E	.	R	. – .
F	. . – .	S	. . .
G	– – .	T	–
H	. . . .	U	. . –
I	. .	V	. . . –
J	. – – –	W	. – –
K	– . –	X	– . . –
L	. – . .	Y	– . – –
M	– –	Z	– – . .